THE FOLLOWER

To the Lavigne family, who let me stay.
R.T.

To Guy and Robin, for friendship and inspiration,
and to Tigger, a cat who walked his own road.
M.S.

First published in the United States in 2000.

Fitzhenry & Whiteside acknowledges with thanks the support of the Government of Canada
through its Book Publishing Industry Development Program.

Fitzhenry & Whiteside acknowledge the support of the Canada Council for the Arts
for our publishing program.

Printed in Hong Kong.
Book Design by Wycliffe Smith.

10 9 8 7 6 5 4 3 2

Canadian Cataloguing in Publication Data

Thompson, Richard, 1951-
The follower

ISBN 1-55041-532-8

1. Children's poetry, Canadian (English).* I. Springett, Martin. II. Title.

PS8589.H53F64 2000   jC811'.54   C00-931120-3
PZ8.3.T46Fo 2000

THE FOLLOWER

Written by Richard Thompson

Illustrated by Martin Springett

Fitzhenry & Whiteside

O**N** Monday,
Dark as shut your eyes,
It followed her home…

Down the lane, over the lawn,
Past the Marble Frog and the Granite Swan.

She cast a glance—and quick as that—
It was gone.

I<small>N</small> Tuesday's fog,
Damp and foul, it followed her home…

Past the graveyard, past the church,
'Neath the skeleton arms of the Hangman's Birch,
Down the lane, over the lawn,
Past the Marble Frog and the Granite Swan.

She turned to look—and quick as that—
It was gone.

*I*N *Wednesday's wind,*
Like a serpent's breath, it followed her home…

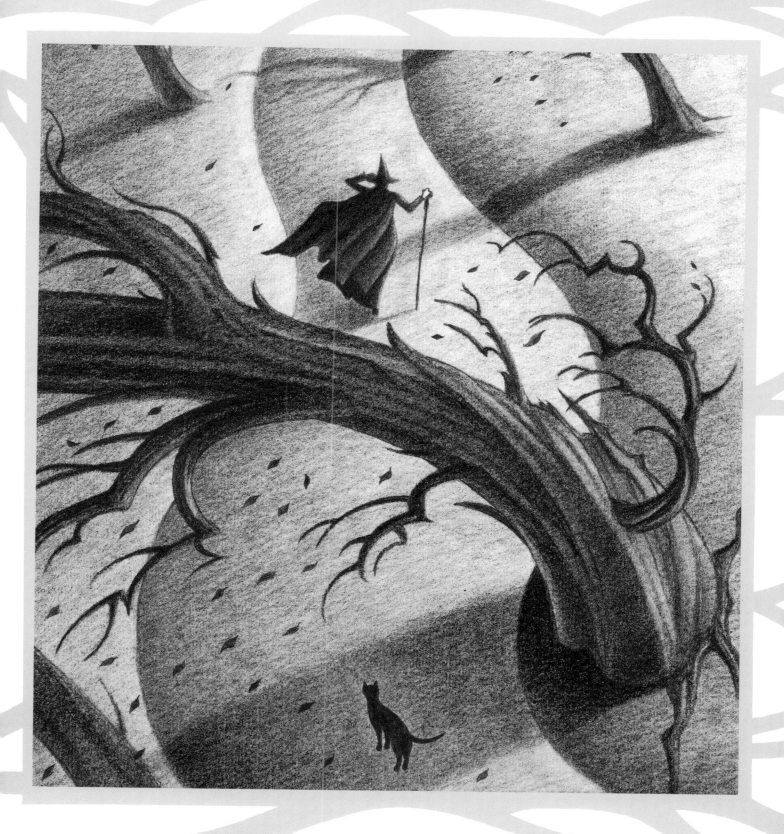

Past the house with the barking dogs,
Along the path through Bogeyman's Bog,
Past the graveyard, past the church,
'Neath the skeleton arms of the Hangman's Birch,
Down the lane, over the lawn,
Past the Marble Frog and the Granite Swan.

She stamped her foot—and quick as that—
It was gone.

*I*n Thursday's storm,
With lightning laced, it followed her home…

Past the mill,
Under the shadow of the Elf King's Hill,
Past the house with the barking dogs,
Along the path through Bogeyman's Bog,
Past the graveyard, past the church,
'Neath the skeleton arms of the Hangman's Birch,
Down the lane, over the lawn,
Past the Marble Frog and the Granite Swan.

She shook her stick—and quick as that—
It was gone.

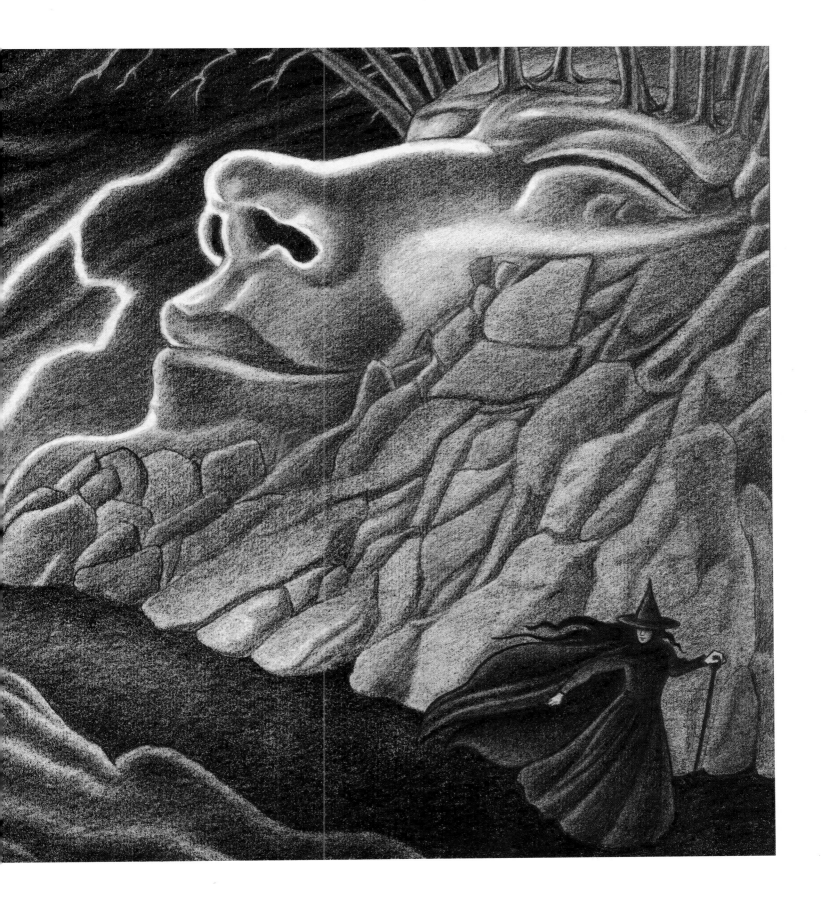

O N Friday,
Under a white stone moon,
It followed her home…

Over the bridge,
Along the ridge,
Past the mill,
Under the shadow of the Elf King's Hill,
Past the house with the barking dogs,
Along the path through Bogeyman's Bog,
Past the graveyard, past the church,
'Neath the skeleton arms of the Hangman's Birch,
Down the lane, over the lawn,
Past the Marble Frog and the Granite Swan.

She spat and hissed—and quick as that—
It was gone.

ON Saturday,
Cold as the ocean's deep,
It followed her home…

Through the forest where the Gunny Wolf lurks,
Past the ruins of the Vinegar Works,
Over the bridge,
Along the ridge,
Past the mill,
Under the shadow of the Elf King's Hill,
Past the house with the barking dogs,
Along the path through Bogeyman's Bog,
Past the graveyard, past the church,
'Neath the skeleton arms of the Hangman's Birch,
Down the lane, over the lawn,
Past the Marble Frog and the Granite Swan.

She said, "Away!"—and quick as that—
It was gone.

O
N Sunday,
Soft with Autumn's sighs,
It followed her home…

Past the cave where the Ogres dwell,
Past the mouth of the Wish-None Well,
Through the forest where the Gunny Wolf lurks,
Past the ruins of the Vinegar Works,
Over the bridge,
Along the ridge,
Past the mill,
Under the shadow of the Elf King's Hill,
Past the house with the barking dogs,
Along the path through Bogeyman's Bog,
Past the graveyard, past the church,
'Neath the skeleton arms of the Hangman's Birch,
Down the lane, over the lawn,
Past the Marble Frog and the Granite Swan.

She said:
"Alright! You win.
I guess you can stay."

It sidled in,
In its sleek sliding way,

And follows her now,
By night and day.